August Rain

Remain blessed!

(signature)

August Rain

GODKULTURE
PUBLISHING

DUNAMIS ORE

August Rain

Paperback ISBN 978-0-9893873-3-0
eBook ISBN 978-0-9893873-4-7
Library of Congress Control Number 2013940139

Published by
GodKulture Publishing
Chicago, Illinois

Phone: 402-419-1072
Email: publishing@Godkulture.org
www.Godkulturepublishing.com

Printed in the United States of America

To everyone
who's ever felt lost in life,
there is hope.

Acknowledgements

God ~ Thank you for EVERYTHING! You rock!!

Dad ~ Thanks for your support. I love you.

Mi madre ~ The mother of all helicopter moms! Thanks for all your support and love.

Nicole ~ Thanks for being my on my side when the boys aren't; you're kinda cool for your age..kinda. Oh, and you still can't have my room after I've left for college!

Casey ~ Thanks for always doing what I ask you to do with no attitude. Thumbs up for being polite and obedient.

Faith ~ I still find it extremely hilarious what you said on my b-day dvd interview and how you said it ;) I'll hold that against you forever, Lol!

Grand-mom ~ Thanks for all your prayers! That's all you literally say everytime you call me or my mom calls. Thank you so much. Hope to see you soon :)

Aunt Sarah & family ~ Thank you guys for all your love, support, and prayers. Much love.

Aunt T & family ~ Thank you so much for all your love and support! God bless.

Amber ~ Thank you so much for everything! I've loved getting to know you more this year and I'm so grateful and blessed to have a friend like you. You're amazing. Thanks for all your support and prayers. Much love and God bless!

Homeschool family at Shabach Christian Academy ~ You guys are awesome! All the students and staff are excellent. Thank you guys for all the love and support. My senior year was one of the best school years I've had. Not only have I been academically successful, but my faith has grown immensely. Special thanks to Ms. Danielle, Mrs. Rorie, Mrs. Onuma, and Ms. Elliott for all your encouraging and lovely words. I'm really going to miss the teachers and students I've worked with in my group classes. It's been an amazing journey.

Mrs. Gibson ~ Thank you for being exceptionally supportive and loving. Your care and understanding has just been phenomenal!

Danielle ~ Thanks for being the amazing friend you are ;)

Britt Nicole ~ I love you!! Your music is brilliant and so inspiring. You're outstanding! God bless.

Cheryl and Demi ~ You two are so inspiring and I love you both. Demi, your strength is amazing and so is your voice! God bless you.

To all the Staff at GodKulture ~ Thank you for a great job.

Contents

Prologue

No one knows what the future has in store. No one knows what could happen tomorrow. Sure I can plan and make my to-do lists but let's face reality here. Life happens and most of the time, even my back up plans can't solve anything. I always complain about life and how unfair it can be sometimes.

It's not my fault. As a human, it's natural for me to complain, even if I have more than enough. I never stop and look around. I never see the extraordinary moments in each ordinary day until something has to wake me up and make me realize that I've been living in my own little world. I've taken the most precious things and people for granted.

There's a little prayer I've heard that says, "God, give us grace to accept with serenity the things that cannot be changed, courage to change the things which should be changed, and the wisdom to distinguish the one from the other." Change is hard to accept, it's difficult to deal with, but it can also be the new beginning you need. Everyone has a life changing story. Here's mine...

Chapter 1

It's the first morning of my sophomore year in high school. During the last school year my dad moved out, my grades dropped, and I lost focus on my music career prep. Today the weather is on my side. Clear blue skies, sunny with just a hint of calm wind. However, it is a new year, and I'm going to make the best of this year with the help of my best friend, Zack. Zack Stallion and I have been the best of friends since preschool. Mom thinks it weird that my best friend is a guy, but I don't think it is. Besides, some girls are too dramatic. They try their best to turn their lives into soap operas. I mean who really cares about some of the crap they talk about. People like Zack and I couldn't care less about that kind of stuff. He's an amazing friend, laid back but hardworking. Cares more about his grades than trying to get a date for Saturday night.

"Lia" mom calls at me. "You can get out now" she says.

"What?" I look at her with a confused face.

Mom's face is like that of most angels I've seen paintings of. Ocean blue eyes, a small narrow nose, and rose pink lips. Her beach blonde wavy hair falls down her back. She used to be a model, but she gave up her career so she could have a family with my dad. Sometimes I feel sorry for her. She had it all. Money, fame, glamour, but had to give it all up because her high school sweetheart wanted to get married, and he didn't want to live in the limelight.

"Have a great first day" she says to me.

"Thanks." I say, getting out of the car.

I walk through the two intimidating forest green doors and the scent of fresh lime hits me. Smells like they used a little too much cleaning product this morning. I quickly walk to my homeroom to avoid passing out from the strong odor. Canyon High isn't your average TV high school where everything looks perfect, but it's good. Even though it's a public school, the janitors keep it squeaky clean. Ninety-four percent is the highest "A" you can earn, and the whole fingertip skirt-dress rule is taken VERY strictly. I guess you could call it one of those posh public schools. The only reason I've put up with all this is because I hate change. Change messes up everything.

"Good morning," a strange voice approaches me, "what's your last name?" I find myself in the doorway of my new homeroom with a teacher greeting me. She's a tall woman with rich dark skin and an executive posture.

"Zebororie" I quickly say.

"Last on the list, here's your schedule." She gives me a piece of paper with a warm smile.

"Thank you, Mrs.…" I pause for her to say her name.

"Swanson" she says. I nod and enter the classroom. This shouldn't take long, so I grab a seat upfront.

"Hey, I'm Britney" the girl next to me says.

"Lia" I tell her.

She has a bright smile showing her pearly teeth and wavy blonde hair just like mom's. I can't help but notice what she's wearing. A bright yellow plain tank with blue jeans short shorts. I wonder if she knows the school dress code. I open *War and Peace* and continue reading from where I stopped last night.

"My family and I moved here from Miami over summer" she says.

"Cool" I tell her looking up from the book.

"So are you new too?"

"No, I've lived here my whole life"

"Wow, so do you like it?"

"Yes, do you mind I'm trying to read here" I say sharply ending the boring conversation. Mrs. Swanson calls for our attention by clapping her hands loudly.

"So future leaders, a new year means new opportunities" she says starting a teacher-to-students lecture. "For those of you who started positively last year and made amazing efforts, please continue or better yet improve your work habits this year for a greater school year."

Her face gets really serious as she pops out her green eyes, squeezes her red hot lips together, and gives a death stare to some students.

"For those of you who spent your freshman skipping classes and doing absolutely NOTHING" she yells scaring most of us, "pick up your slack because if you're not ready to work this year you can as well never show up to school again. I'm still dumbfounded about how some of you managed not to get held back."

She asks if we have any questions, but no one has the courage to speak. When Mrs. Swanson returns to her desk, Britney asks me what classes I have. I casually tell her my classes starting with first period.

"Wow" she says, "wait, you said health, calculus, and AP English are your first three classes right?"
"Yeah." I give her my schedule for her to see.

She looks at it making an enormous "O" with her mouth. She looks down at what I think is my last class and is about to scream when she remembers Mrs. "No Nonsense" is in the room.
"What?" I ask.
"I'm in four of your classes" she shrieks.

I check her schedule to make sure and see that

she is right. Great! Just what I need. A happy go lucky teenager who dresses like a twelve year old, to be in over half of my classes. I look up at her and see she's wearing her huge annoying smile. She starts talking about how we can study together, and hang out together after school or something like that. I totally tune out and start writing lyrics in my head – something I do when bored. Britney figures out I'm not listening and starts waving her hands frantically in front of my face until I tell her to please stop.

The school announcement comes on and I thank them. Today, they're really slow and boring because it's the first day. After welcoming freshmen, new students, and students who came back, they start talking about the new clubs students can join. Then Mr. Pike, the principal, comes on the screen and gives a speech to us about how we should set new goals for ourselves. I swear that man is a pervert. Looking at him gives me the creeps, so I pull out my book and read till the announcements are over. The bell rings and Mrs. Swanson wishes us a great first day. As I walk to health class I get the feeling I'm being followed but every time I turn around, no one's behind me. I hurry and make my way to class. So far sophomore year is not going so well.

I'm about to enter health when Britney jumps out of nowhere giving me a mini-heart attack. She was the one following me. She laughs at the fact that she scared me. So childish. I ignore her walking into class.

The next few hours drag on crazily. It's impossible to concentrate when most of these teachers are so boring. It's the same thing in every class. The rules, procedures, introductions, what they like to do in their personal time. I'm here to learn. I really don't care about whether you like to draw animals or go shopping with your teenage daughters. I hope I don't die of boredom this year.

Lunch finally arrives and I go outside to wait under the large oak tree in the school's front lawn. Zack and I ate lunch every day here last year unless it rained, which it barely did. I'm sitting under it when I see someone who looks like Britney coming to my direction. I look a little closer and see that it is her. How on earth could this girl possibly find me. I know I didn't tell her where I was going to be during lunch. I have a personal stalker. Thanks Canyon High for this welcome back to school gift.

"What are you doing here and how did you find me?" I ask standing up when she gets closer.

"Just wanted to have lunch with you"

"Okay, well how did you find me?"

"I asked people," she says. "You know you're really popular around here."

I want to tell her to go away, but Zack finally arrives and gives me a bear hug. I look up into his blue eyes and smile. The way they sparkle always make me smile.

"What took you so long?" I ask.

"I had to turn in work to some of my teachers" he says removing his backpack.

"What work?" I ask. "Today's the first day back."

"You get extra credit for doing work over summer, my friend"

"You are one weird guy." I remember Britney is standing next to me. "Speaking of weirdos, Zack this is Britney"

"Oh my, Lia you didn't tell me about him" she says.

"What are you talking about?" I ask her.
Her annoying smile pops up on her face again. "Why didn't you tell me you have a boyfriend?"
"What?" Zack and I say in unison. My eyes bulge out and my fingers form a fist.
"He is NOT my boyfriend" I tell her angrily. "You are so ignorant, guys and girls can just be friends you know."

I hate it when people think like that. She says she's sorry so we sit down and eat in silence until Zack asks her where she's from. They start a conversation I take no part in. It's bad enough I have four classes with the bizarre girl, I really don't want to have lunch with her. Her annoying laugh starts to irritate me. I've had enough of this so I get up and tell them I'm going to the library.
"Can we come with you?" Britney asks.
"No, you kids just stay and enjoy your lunch" I tell both of them, rolling my eyes at Britney.

The rest of my classes are almost as boring as my morning ones. By the time the last bell rings I feel a rush of relief. I hurry out to avoid seeing Britney again, knowing she was in my last class.

Mom and I get home thirty minutes later because of traffic which gave us time to talk about my day and Britney. Home, sweet, home is deep in one of the forests Phoenix has. It's a simple four bedroom house in which I've lived in all my life. This is the only house I know, it's my only home. I love the fact that it's away from society. It's a very secluded house. We don't have any neighbors yelling at us or little kids running around. Since I'm not a people person this is the perfect kind of house for me.

"I'm going to my room working on music, so please try not to need me" I tell mom as I jog onto the stairs.

My room is my personal sanctuary. There are no posters of anyone or anything. It isn't colorful or childish. The only splash of color in here are cream colored curtains. It's peaceful and serene. I trade my school bag for my guitar. A plain and old but functional guitar. My parents gave me the treasure on my eighth birthday. I call my guitar my guitar, not lulu or Cynthia or anything like that. I grab a blank music sheet from a folder on my nightstand, sit on my bed, and start writing. For me, writing gives me the daily rush I need to survive. Not writing is like not breathing. The way the words bounce off the pages and into my heart with the beautiful melody surrounding it is just extraordinary. Music is a universal language the world speaks, but to me it's also my life.

Two hours have passed and I'm still writing. My phone vibrates showing an unfamiliar number.

"Hello?"

"Hi Lia, its Britney from school" She says in a perky voice.

"How did you get my number?"

"Zack gave it to me."

"Why?"

"Because I asked for it."

"Why?"

"Hey, what's with all the questions?" she replies.

"What do you want?" I sharply ask her. I seriously don't have time for this.

"Just wanted to say hi"

"Okay, hi .... bye"

"Wait, what are you doing?"

I tell her I'm writing a song then hang up. That might be rude but I don't have time to waste. I can't concentrate anymore so I go downstairs to set the table for dinner. It takes me almost twenty minutes to set the table mom's way. She is such a perfectionist. Everything has to be good or bad; there's no almost with her. I let out a squeal when mom brings out what we're having.

Usually we have tofu with vegetables, which is totally unsatisfying and since mom has always being a vegan I am too because of her. The plates are filled with creamy mashed potatoes; white wine shell pasta stuffed with rich mozzarella cheese covered in our family's one-of-a-kind mouthwatering pasta sauce with a special ingredient mom has never mentioned. She tells me that we're going to have to spend two extra hours at gym on Saturday, and I tell her I'm perfectly okay with that.

The doorbell rings and mom rushes to the door. Now I know why we're having a feast instead of the usual inadequate meal. She comes into the dining room with Emily, my older sister who should be in Berkley.
"Hey" I say hugging her, "How was Europe?"
"Awesome, I'll show you some pictures later" She says in her sweet voice.
Emily got to spend the summer in Europe by telling mom that it's either she would go to Cambridge (since she also got accepted there) or she could go to the UC Berkley, but mom would have to let her spend the summer alone in Europe and with mom being the helicopter parent that she is, Emily got to go to Europe. I ask her why she's here and not in California.
"My classes don't start till the next two weeks" She replies eyeing the table. We sit and start eating the delectable food while mom sticks with her tofu.
After dinner I tell them goodnight and go to bed getting enough sleep for another day of dread. This day

didn't turn out exactly like I had planned and I have a feeling tomorrow's not going to be any different.

The next day at lunch I decide to go to the school's library so I don't I have to pretend that I like Britney. So far I haven't talked to her in any of my classes and I don't plan on it. Zack and Britney walk into the library.

"What are you guys doing here?" I ask whispering.

"We just wanted to see if you're okay" Zack says. He starts searching my eyes to find out what's wrong.

"I'm fine, thanks for checking" I tell both of them and furiously exit the library. I hear them coming after me.

"What's up with you today?" Zack asks me when he and the blonde catch up with me. He looks at me with a worried expression.

"Nothing, I'm just having a bad day" I tell him walking as fast as I can in the opposite direction. A few seconds later I turn around only to see Zack walking the other way with Britney. My heart sinks a little.

After a horrible day in school I'm just glad to be home. I sense something is wrong when I see my sister and two women in the living room. When I ask Emily why they are here, she tells me that she and mom are concerned about me and they thought if I didn't want to talk to them, maybe I could talk to the counselors. I look at the women and they smile at me. Then I look at my sister and mom, tell them that I don't need anyone to talk to and go to my room, slamming the door behind me. I can't believe they called counselors for me, like I'm some kind of psycho who needs to let out her feelings and tell complete strangers everything about her life. Why can't they just accept that I'm an independent person? If I'm going through trauma, which I'm not, I can handle it on my own. I don't need anyone's help, and I never will. I lay on my bed and close my eyes, escaping into my dreams and away from the troubles of reality.

After waking up I get my homework. I start talking to my dad, this makes me a little crazy, but that's just the way it is. Every day, for an hour or two, I talk to him about my day and ask him questions. Though I have no idea where he is or why he left. It's hard for me to admit that I miss him because that's the way I am. I put on a tough face and build walls around myself so I don't get hurt by people. I am headstrong, but that doesn't mean I don't break down behind closed doors. I like being alone and doing things on my own, but when you do that for a while, life kind of gets lonely. However I can't change because the nicest people are the ones others usually take advantage of and I'm not going to let anyone take advantage of me in any way. People from school always ask me why I act the way I do and I always tell them love me or hate me, I don't care because that is who I am and this is who I'll ever be, so get used to it. Some of them listen and get it and others ignore. I've gone through too much to worry about what people think of me. The only opinion that matters is mine.

Mom thought it would be delightful to have Zack and his family over for dinner which by the way is not what I needed considering the way I acted towards him earlier today. After eating, Zack asks his mom if he and I can go outside for a while. Unfortunately his mom says yes, but we have to be back soon since it's a school night. We start walking into my backyard which is in the woods and I know exactly where we're going.

It takes us a few minutes to get to our destination. Behind the trees in the pine green forest is the most beautiful lake I've ever seen and the cool thing is Zack and I are the only ones who know about this place. This is where we usually come to hang out, talk, or just get away from everything. The clear blue lake is sparkling with the sun's help today. Surrounded by clear skies, jade-colored shaggy trees reaching up to six feet, and spiky but glossy white hard rocks, it's the perfect place for me to clear out my head. The scent of refreshing water fills the atmosphere. Even though it's almost seven o' clock, the sun is still up and the weather is bright and breezy. Today was one of perfect weather days for kite flying. The lake is the focal point of everything which makes me feel calm and centered whenever I'm here.

"So what's wrong?" Zack asks leaning on the back of one of the trees.

I thought he had forgotten about today, but I guess not. I'm not sure if I should tell him, but he's my best friend he'll understand, right? Besides, we've never kept anything from each other. He's willing to listen and I need someone to talk to. In addition he's the only one I truly trust, so I spill out everything. I tell him about how much I miss my dad and how crazy things have been since he left. I tell him about how I've been trying to focus on music to forget about everything that's going on and I also tell him how much I can't stand his perky new blonde friend. I finally stop talking and for a while, all we can hear is the wind whistling. When he sees the tears slowly coming down my face, he extends his arms to hug me, then tells me he's going to be there for me and everything will be okay. Just what I need to hear, now if only I can believe it.

All of a sudden it starts drizzling. Then rain starts pouring down. The fact that it's August and rain is coming down like this is extremely bizarre since there hasn't been a drop of rain this summer. I start walking towards the house when Zack grabs my hand, holding me back.

"Dance with me" he says.

"Are you crazy, we're going to get soaked" I tell him.

"Lia, when was the last time it rained like this?" he asks.

No answer.

He takes my hand and we literally start dancing in the August rain. As crazy we look right now, I'm enjoying this moment. While dancing, we both transform into the little kids we once were. Back when life was free of troubles and the only responsibility we had was to have fun. He lifts and twirls me. I feel safe and secured in his arms. Nothing can touch me. Looking into his ocean blue eyes, my fears and worries diminish. When the rain stops, I ask him to promise he's never going to let anyone or anything get in the way of our friendship. "I will never let anything or anyone get in the way of our friendship." He says. "I promise you Lia, when I can I'll always be there for you and I'll never leave you crying. You know I keep my promises."

I nod and he gives me a hug before we head back to my house.

Chapter 2

"I'll miss you so much Lia, take care of mom for me" Emily says.

Mom and I are dropping her off at the airport a few days earlier than planned so she can get to California on time. We hug, then she and mom hug. We say our goodbyes to Emily and in the blink of an eye she's gone. "How about going out for dinner?" mom asks as we walk out to the car.

"Yeah, sure"

Now that classes are getting out of summer mode, and into work zone the teachers are giving us students a lot more homework. When I get home from school I barely have time to work on music. The work teachers give us is too much. First they assign us dozens of essays, reports, and study packets to fill out. Then they complain and grumble about not getting enough sleep because they were up all night grading our work. I definitely think the law of moderation should also apply to homework. If only teachers and students could switch roles for a week, maybe just maybe they could know how we feel.

"Lia, Zack is here" mom yells to me from the front door.

Most kids my age are taking their little siblings out for trick or treat tonight, that is if they themselves aren't taking part in the childish tradition. Regardless here I am by myself , trying to figure out what I'm going to do with the lyrics I've written. I guess now that Zack's here, I won't be so lonely. I rush to the front door and see Zack with Britney standing on my front steps. What a surprise. Without letting them in, I immediately ask what Britney is doing at my house. Zack answers for her, saying she just wanted to hang out with us. Whatever, what could she possibly do wrong that that would tick me off tonight. We make our way to the music room and I ask Zack if he could help me with the music for my lyrics.

"Sure which one?" he asks. I hand him a music sheet with scribbles and words crossed. His eyes widen when he sees it.

"Yeah, I kept changing my mind" I say red-faced.

"I didn't know you write songs, that's so cool" Britney tells me.

"Thanks." I say. This girl might not be bad news after all.

We're working hard on the song when Zack points out it's getting late. We both agree to continue working on it some other time.

"What are we going to do now?" Britney asks.

I suggest watching a movie until Zack's mom comes to pick them. When I pick one of my favorites, *The Dark Knight*, Britney lets out a squeal.

"That's one of my favorite movies" she says looking like a six year old on Christmas morning.

"Really?" Zack asks, "You don't look like that type of girl." He has an innocent look on his face like he doesn't know he just said something offensive, which of course he doesn't because he's a guy and most guys are like that.

"Just because I wear pink skirts and floral dresses, put on lip gloss with glitter and hate when my nail breaks doesn't mean I don't like movies with car chases" she tells him in a defending tone.

I give her a hi-5 as Zack apologizes to her. We grab some organic, tasteless popcorn (it's either this or tofu) and watch the last of Heath Ledger's movies. Halfway through the Dark Knight, Zack's mom comes to pick them up.

"It was really fun hanging out with you" Britney says. "At least now I know you don't completely hate me."

"You're not so bad yourself" I tell her. "You're not as annoying as I thought you would be." Mom and Zack both give me a loathsome look.

"It's okay, I get that a lot" she says. "Goodnight" She hugs me and walks out the door. I kind of feel sorry for her now, she was just trying to make some new friends and I was being cold to her.

"Hey Britney, if you ever need a friend to talk to or hang out with" I say, "You can always call me."

"Thanks" she says smiling.

After they leave, mom tells me how proud she is of me. I am too. For some reason, there's this feeling I can't describe when you've done something to put a smile on someone's face. It's like a little glow igniting in your heart. Right now I feel that glow, and it's amazing.

"Do you have any plans for Christmas?" Britney asks me. We're both shopping for last minute presents in Hollister. Even though the weather here doesn't reflect that it's December, we only have two more days before Christmas.

"Not really, I'm just going to watch holiday movies with mom and sister while eating cookies and drinking strawberry milkshakes" I tell her.

"Oh" she says handing me a shirt she thinks Emily will like. I take it from her looking at the price and find it surprisingly affordable.

"Why are you asking?"

"I was thinking that if you and your family don't mind, maybe you guys and Zack's family can spend Christmas with my family."

"Sure I'll ask my mom and sister" I tell her heading over to the cashier.

"What about your dad?" she asks innocently.

This is kind of awkward considering I haven't told her much about my family since we became friends.

"He doesn't celebrate Christmas with us anymore" I say, "My dad left a few months ago." Better to rip off the bandage than to beat around the bush.

"I'm sorry" she says.
I tell her it's fine and we pay for the stuff we picked. This Christmas has officially made me bankrupt.

"Merry Christmas" I say to mom in the living room before going to check what's under the tree.
"Merry Christmas Lia."
"Where's Emily?"
"At the airport"

I give mom a strange look and she clarifies by telling me Emily is picking up her boyfriend. Since when did Emily get a boyfriend and why does she have a boyfriend, but most importantly why is she picking him up from the airport. As I try to answer the questions, Emily bursts into the living room wishing mom and I merry Christmas. She then introduces us to her boyfriend, Ben.

"Merry Christmas Mrs. Zebororie and to you Lia" he says.

"Amelia" I correct him. He doesn't know me well enough to start calling me Lia.

"Mom, we have to get to the church on time so we don't miss the service" I tell her and then go to my room without making Ben feel welcomed, because he's not.

While putting on jewelry in front of my mirror, I look at my reflection for a minute. I don't recognize the girl staring back at me. Someone else is who I see. A girl with fear in her sorrowful brown eyes and facial expressions that shows weakness and vulnerability. I know I'm not the person I see. I'm much stronger than she is. I'm prettier than she is. Right? I break down into tears and see that I'm not as strong as I thought I was. I am vulnerable and weak. To the bottom left is a picture of my dad and I's last Christmas. It's the only one I have of him since mom burnt all the other pictures of him. I wipe my tears and hurry back downstairs. Ben and Emily decide to come with us. Surprising because Emily's not the religious type. Really none of us are. We're going to the service because Britney invited us. Anyway we all get into the car and I tell mom to step on it, because we're running late. When we get to the church, we're greeted by Britney and her family.

"Merry Christmas" Britney says cheerfully hugging me.

"Merry Christmas Britney" I reply "This is for you."

I give her a small pink gift bag. She anxiously removes a jewelry box and opens it, finding a silver ruby-heart charm bracelet. After thanking me, she gives me a black bag with pink ribbons. I look inside and pull out my present: all my music sheets creatively binded together like a book.

"Don't worry I didn't touch your originals, Zack photocopied them for me" she says.

I thank her and we go in to the sanctuary with our families. Britney finds Zack and his family so we sit next to them. He asks me in a quiet voice if I'm okay. I nod yes. As the service starts, tears roll down my cheeks. I quickly wipe them so no one sees them, but I know Zack saw my tears because he whispers in my ear, "Everything will be okay."

Zack gives me my present after a day full of fun. I thank him and give him his little present. We say our goodbyes and my family and I go home.

I head straight for my room when we get home without saying a word to mom or Emily. I'm angry at Emily for bringing her colorless boyfriend home for a holiday that's special to our family and I'm angrier at mom for letting her bring him and not even telling me about him. Sometimes she gets me so irritated. I climb into bed, trying my best to forget about all that drama and relive the fun moments I had with Britney and Zack today. I carefully remove the wrap from the Zach's present. Opening the box, I bring out a scrapbook. I know he made this because it looks homemade plus he knows I love homemade presents. The cover says Memories in big, blue bold letters. I flip open the pages and see pictures of just the two of us or both of us with our families and friends with hilarious captions underneath. I laugh when I see the picture of us at the car wash to raise money for our school last year. We have soap all over our hands and faces. I turn the page and tears fill up my eyes as I stare at a picture of both our families together. Back when everything was normal and okay. I go through the rest of the scrapbook passing silly, sad, weird, and out of the blue photos. On the last page of the memory book, I see a note from Zack.

Hey Lia, hope you love the scrapbook. This book isn't only filled with words & pictures, but it's also filled with many memories. Some are great, others not so much. Some are priceless and others are just so weird. The point is we have been through so much together over the years and to see you grow into the determined and dedicated person you've become has been amazing. I'm very thankful I have the chance to know someone like you. Even though your family went through a rough time last year, you remained strong and hopeful. I'm proud of you for giving Britney a chance. Both of you have turned out to be great friends. You have to stop worrying about your dad. Time heals all wounds and you may not believe me now but everything will soon be okay. You'll be all right. I love you Lia.

I put the scrapbook safely on my nightstand and even though I don't want to cry, tears fall onto my pillow gently.

Chapter 3

"Oh my gosh," Britney says, "it's beautiful."
Zack and I brought her down to see the enchanted lake
scenery in the forest behind my house. This officially
makes her a best friend of mine. I can't believe I'm
saying this, but it's fun having a girl my age as a friend.
There are so many things I talk to her about that I
would never feel comfortable talking to Zack or mom
with. Not to mention we like most of the same movies,
books, and sports. I tell her she has to keep this place a
secret and she says she will. We all sit down against the
trees and Britney and I talk about how uncoordinated
our Spanish teacher is while Zack just listens. We then
decide to play who, what, where or when and Britney
volunteers to be the first victim. She picks what, so I
ask her what is the worst thing that has ever happened
to her. Zack elbows me saying I should pick another
question, but I tell him no and wait for Britney's answer.
She has an uneasy look on her face. Zack tells her she
doesn't have to answer the question. She looks down

and asks if Zack and I are truly her friends. We both answer yes.

"You guys would never tell a friend's secret, right?" she asks still looking down.

"Whatever it is Britney, you can trust us." I assure her "We won't tell a soul."

"Okay." She begins. "My older brother had this friend. They were like the best of friends and both of our families had known each other for a long time and were comfortable with each other. Well, my parents went on a fourth honeymoon two years ago during spring break, so my brother had to come home from his freshman year of college to stay with me. It was a Saturday afternoon that his friend came over and when my brother had to run some errands, so he left me home alone with him. Later that day, he raped me. I was only thirteen."

My eyes widen at the sound of those words and teardrops roll down her cheeks as she looks up at us. I move closer to her and hold her in my arms as she cries. Zack tells her he's extremely sorry.

"Why are you so sorry?" she asks wiping her face, "You weren't the one who hurt me"

He doesn't answer fearing he might say something wrong. I however, look straight into her eyes and ask if she told her parents. She nods and I ask her what they did or said.

"Forgive and forget" she says.

"What?" I ask in an annoyed tone. "The guy assaulted you and that's all they could say. Did you even take him to court?"

"His parents are close friends with mine. I couldn't have taken him to court even if I wanted to. His parents apologized to my family and I and made us promise not to take them to court."

"So you just sat there and stayed quiet?" I ask.

"Lia, what else could I do" she says in an upset tone. "I was only thirteen, it wasn't like I could get myself a lawyer and charge him." She calms down and stands up.

"When something like that happens to you" she says to me, "the best thing you can do to help yourself is forgive."

"Forgive?" I ask her like I've never heard of the word before.

"Yes," she says, "forgive. Forgive yourself for the hatred you gave yourself and thinking it was your fault or you could have done something to prevent the tragedy. Forgive the person or people who hurt you deeply because that's the first step towards the healing process and forgive the witnesses. The people who saw you grieving, but never stopped by to help. They saw you hurting, but never asked why."

It takes a little while for me to completely take in what she says. Then I tell her it isn't that easy to just forgive, neither is easy to forget everything that happened.

"Of course I didn't forget," she explains. "If I did would I be telling it to you now?"

"No" I whisper. I look over at Zack. He hasn't said a word since Britney started talking about forgiveness.

"Look, I was furious when all my parents said to me was to forgive and forget because to forgive is one thing, but to forget is just impossible, especially when a special part of you has been stripped away and you know you can never get it back."

She looks straight ahead at the horizon.

"I've learned the earlier you forgive, the earlier you'll heal. In addition, I know God didn't send His only Son, Jesus, to die for me to live a life of pain and hatred." She turns around and looks me in the eye. "He died so I could live a life full of joy, happiness, peace, and eternity."

"So you're a Jesus freak?" I ask her standing up.

"Yes, I am," she says. "What do you know Jesus freaks?"

"I know most of them are really annoying" I say truthfully.

"Why?"

"Because all they ever talk about is Jesus and how good God is"

"Why does that annoy you?"

"Because it's NOT TRUE" I say angrily, "If God

is as good as you Christians say then why are all these bad things happening, why are innocent people dying every day? Why are there so-called Christians spreading hate instead of love? Why did something so horrible even happen to you, a Jesus freak?"

"Because life happens" she says, "things happen that are supposed to test your faith, they happen to remind you that God is still God no matter what anyone thinks, to make you see that you can't help yourself. Stuff, even the bad ones happen to glorify God."

At this point I'm beyond angry. All this religious crap Britney said is starting to get on my nerves. I don't know what she's trying to prove, but she's not convincing me. She literally just told me that my dad leaving is glorifying God. How on earth am I supposed to believe God even cares when my family isn't together anymore.

"Lia, I'm not afraid to say it" she continues, "most people think when something unfortunate happens to them, it's either that someone's out to get them or God hates them" she smiles at Zack who is also standing now and then back at me. "People will say anything, but it doesn't matter because if your heart is with God, the pain that you may be feeling now cannot and will not compare to the joy that's afterward."

Zack and I look at each other, then at Britney. I tell her I have no idea what she's talking about. She tells me to think about it and just like that, she leaves.

Zack and I watch her walk back to my house alone. I don't agree with her, but I have to admire her courage and way of living. After all she's been through, she's still doing her best to put a smile on the faces of people.

"Hey, remember when Britney started talking about God and Jesus and how they want us to be happy?" Zack asks.

Britney left about three hours earlier and we're setting the table for dinner. I nod and he continues by asking me if I think it's true.

"Do you think she's telling the truth?" he asks me.

"About what?"

"About God, Jesus, forgiveness" he says.

"Honestly, I don't know. You and I both know how bad I hate religious stuff. Going to church on Christmas doesn't make me a Christian. My family doesn't even really celebrate the holiday religiously. I don't care about Buddhism, Islam, Judaism, Christianity, or anything else the world has to offer. How on earth would I know if Britney's telling the truth? I bet you if we talked to a Muslim or Buddhist, they would tell us their religion is the right one. That's why I stay out of religion. It's like they all want something from you, you know?"

"I'm sorry, but haven't you ever wondered if there's more to life than we think. I mean what if someone we love died, would they go to heaven, hell or is there no heaven --"

"Stop it okay." I cut him off irritated. "Just forget about what Britney said. I don't need any of my loved ones dead." The conversation ends on that note.

While eating dinner that evening I ponder on what Zack asked me. Is there really more to life or I'm I just letting Zack and Britney feed me lies.

On Monday afternoon, I see Britney heading towards me in the school hallway, so I pull out a book from my bag to avoid her. Apparently she doesn't get the message and says hi.

"Morning Britney" I say putting my book down. She tells me that Zack came to her church yesterday and he had fun with the youth group. I ask myself why Zack would go and my conscience tells me he went to get answers for all those questions he was asking. "That's great" I tell Britney with a fake smile.

"Yeah," she says, "he asked many questions."

"What are you doing over spring break?" I ask, quickly changing the subject.

"Not much" she says, "Why?"

I tell her I'm just asking even though the real reason was to shut her up about church. I just don't need any of that in my life, especially now that it is getting normal again. We walk out of the school building breathing in the fresh air. Spring greets me with a full week of no school and homework.

Three days into spring break and I'm already

bored. After writing everything I can, I have writer's block. I called Zack last night and he told me he couldn't come over because he and Britney are doing something in church today. Something about empowering younger teens. Great just what I needed, another Jesus freak. It's like Britney is trying to steal him from me. Zach and I are just friends, why would she need to "steal" him from me. She might not even like him in that way. Besides, she's a saint. I take a warm bath instead of a shower to relax and clear my head of all negative thoughts. I decide to watch some TV downstairs when I'm done. When I enter the living room, I see mom on the phone. She looks like she just saw a ghost. When she gets off the phone, I immediately ask her what' wrong.

"That was Zack's mom I was on the phone with" she says slowly.

"What did she say?" I ask anxiously. She looks at me, then tells me sit down and I do.

"What did she say?" I ask again trying to be calm.

"On his way back home from the church event he went for, Zach was involved in" she pauses then slowly says, "an extremely terrible accident."

I feel like I really did, just crashed and burned. I ask mom if she is serious and unfortunately she is.

"What about Britney?" I ask still trying to be calm.

"She was in another car."

"Where is he?" I ask, "I mean which hospital is

he in?"

"I don't know sweetie."

"Well, call his mom back and let's go" I say taking command. She asks me if I want to change first. I tell her no. There's no time to change. I leave the house in my robe and comfy room slippers. We get into the car as mom gets the hospital information from Zack's mom.

When we get there I ask if he's okay but no one answers me. I ask again. Still no answer. Fearing the worst, I barge myself into his hospital room before anyone can hold me back. I run to his bedside and explode into tears. Lightning strikes me when I see him breathless making me fall to my knees. Mom and Zack's parents try to pick me up, but I don't let them. I hold on to one of his lifeless hands. They try to remove my hand from his, but I hold on as hard as I can.

"Stop trying to separate us" I yell at them.

"You have to let go" mom says.

"I can't, never."

Zack's dad decides to lift me up while mom tries to separate Zack and I. I fight each of them with everything I have left in me. I can't leave. I won't leave. They finally get me to sit down steadily in the waiting area. When all is done and all is said, mom drives me back home. We get home later than expected. I sluggishly climb the stairs and dump myself on the bed. Mom says she'll stay in here until I fall asleep to make sure I'm okay, but I tell her she can go. Right now I just want to be alone. When she leaves, little droplets of clear liquid start to roll down again. I put both of my hands on my heart to feel the heartbeat and close my eyes.

Chapter 4

This morning everything seems blurry. I get up to draw my curtains. It's too bright in here. After adjusting the curtains, I climb back into bed. I don't have any intentions of getting out of bed today. No intentions of seeing anyone or going anywhere. No intentions of being happy. How can I even be happy when my best friend is gone? He left the world leaving me behind. The one person I love the most in the world is gone and he's never coming back. How am I supposed to live without him? How am I to go day by day without hearing his voice? He promised me to be there for me whenever I needed him. He promised he'd never leave me crying. Now I'm drowning in tears and he's not here. I close my eyes and instantly see his comforting face. I open my eyes to avoid seeing the illusion. Holding on to my heart, I try to keep it from hurting but the pain remains. Mom comes in with a bowl of fruit salad, what I eat when I'm not in a great mood. The last thing on my mind right now is food. I tell her I'm not hungry and she should please leave.

"You have to eat something," she says, "It's almost two o'clock and you haven't eaten anything today." She sets the bowl on my nightstand and sits on my bed.

"Why didn't you tell me before we got to the hospital?"

"I didn't know how to" she says. "Britney called."

"Why?"

"She wanted to check if you were okay."

She gets up telling me I should call her if I need anything and leaves. Right after she leaves, I open the bottom drawer of the nightstand and pull out the scrapbook. The scrapbook Zack filled with the best recollections of life's wonderful moments. As I go through the pages, I reminisce over the memories. Strangely enough, this time I'm not crying.

"What on earth are you doing here?" It's 10 pm and Britney's in my doorway.

"I wanted to see how you were doing" she says, coming in.

"As you can clearly see, I'm fine." I look at her with hatred and tell her to leave.

"I'm really sorry about Zack."

"You should be."

"What's that supposed to mean?" She asks infuriated.

"Don't be idiotic with me Britney." I struggle to get out of bed with every ounce of energy I have left. I get in her face fearless.

"You are the reason Zack died and you know it" I yell to her face.

"No I'm not, I had nothing to do with it" she yells back. I've never seen her so furious.

"Save the lies for someone else, Britney" I say violently, "You and I both know that he got involved in the accident while on his way back home from a stupid church event that you invited him to."

"He wasn't the only one in the car, Lia" she shouts at me.

"Yes, but he was the only one who died."

I am very irritated with her right now. I just want her to leave and never come back. That way, I don't have to see her ignorant, deceiving, hypocritical, conniving little face anymore. I get back into my bed.

"I am not to blame for what happened," she says, "say what you want to say and do what you want, but you know in your heart that it's not my fault."

"Whatever."

"I know how upset you are" she says in a calm voice, "he was my friend too."

"You think just because you were friends with him for a few months, he's your best friend?" I look at her and say, "You didn't even know him."

She walks out sobbing and before she slams my door, I ask her why her God watched my friend die and why she believes in a God that doesn't even exist.

Saturday afternoon, I wake up to find mom with a guy downstairs. She sees me and introduces us. I politely shake his hand while mom tells me his name is Harry. He's one tall man, but with a weird posture. Wears the strangest pair of glasses I've ever seen. I ask him what he does for a living and he tells me he's a neurosurgeon. Figured. I look at mom staring at him. I never knew she went for doctors. Well, it's been a while since she had a man in her life. I guess even old people get lonely.

Harry joins us for dinner, but all I think about is the argument Britney and I had last night. Who does she think she is, telling me that she knows how I feel and that none of what happened was her fault. She has only been friends with Zack for a few months, I have been his best friend for years. How dare her tell me she knows how I feel. The guts of some people.

Mom is letting me stay home from school today because she thinks I'm can't go back to school yet. I go into the music room and see Harry touching my instruments, pens, pencils. He starts looking through the music sheets I left in here. I hate it when people touch my stuff, especially without my permission.

"What are you doing?" I ask trying not to yell. Apparently I kind of scared him.

"I was just..." he hesitates. He smiles, but I don't see anything worth smiling about.

"...touching my stuff without my permission." I

finish the sentence for him.

"I'm sorry..." he says, "but you better start giving your future stepdad respect." I rush to the kitchen to find mom.

"The freak that had dinner with us last night is saying he's my new stepdad" I say.

"Amelia, show some respect."

Harry comes in and I ask mom what on earth is going on.

"Harry and I have been dating for a while now," she says holding his hand, "and last night after you went to bed, he proposed!"

"Wait when did you guys start dating?" I ask horrified.

"That doesn't matter," she says, "we're going to be a family." I pull her away into the living room where Harry can't hear us.

I take a deep breath, then explode.

"Okay," I say, "WHAT THE HELL ARE YOU DOING?"

"Don't you dare use that tone with me Lia" she says in a serious tone.

"Fine just tell me why you started dating him and I met him for the first time the same night he proposed. Are you seriously going to get married again so soon?"

"Look it's my life, my family"

"I'm not going to be part of the family if you marry him"

"Which family will you be part of, where will you live?"

she asks looking me dead in the eyes.

"Why are you doing this?" I ask with tears building up. She sits and looks down, avoiding eye contact with me. "Your father left us with not only pain but lot of debt," she says still looking down, "and we're slowly running out of cash." I take a minute to process this information. "So you're getting married to him for money?"

"No, I'm not" she says, "He's a great man plus it's either this or you have to get a job."

I tell her to look me straight in eyes and she does. I take a step closer to get in her personal space.

"You disgust me" I spit out.

I need some air. On my way out, I see Harry and tell him we don't need his money. I would rather get a job than to let someone replace my father. I go outside and try to cool off. First my dad leaves, then my best friend dies. Now my insane and heartless mom is engaged to someone I met yesterday. Why is she doing this to me? If only Zack was here. I could have talked to him about this. I start to run. My feet don't know where they're going, but my heart does. I keep running till I reach my destination. Falling to the ground, I look over at the lake. I haven't been here since Britney told Zack and I her secret. As I stare into the lake, dozens of memories hit me and even though I'm trying to be strong, innocent tears fall. I quickly wipe them.

How can someone just go and never come back? He was right here, beside me a week ago. I talked to him on the phone the night before he died not knowing I would never hear his comforting voice ever again. I stand and go into the lake, uniting myself with the ice cold water and travel back in time.

After the sun goes down, I get out of the lake and sit on the dry grass nearby. Why is mom doing this to me, why is she doing this to herself? Why, Zach did you leave, I ask out loud looking up at the stars. I stay silent for a while and just think. I think about everything that has happened and is happening. Why me, why now. My dad leaving was bad enough, now my best friend is dead and mom is getting married to a stranger for his money. What did I do to deserve this much pain and agony? Never have I been so confused and terrified. I glance at my reflection in the lake. Puffy eyes and a red face is all I see. I don't know what else to do so I scream. I scream at the top of my lungs letting out the anger and frustration in my head. I scream to let out the hopelessness and hatred in my heart. Love and peace no more abide in me. While trying to let out my frustration, I find a twig. I sharpen it with a rough small stone and play with the idea of torturing my skin with it. I hold my right arm up to the light provided by the stars and lightly touch it with the sharpened twig. The sharp object creates a mind of its own and starts moving up and down my arm a little restlessly, slowly letting out little droplets of red liquid. It becomes violent and more blood comes out. I don't stop the twig, I have no power over it. As the blood starts to gush out, I feel a rush of adrenaline. Tears come down my cheeks not because my arm hurts, but my heart is aching. The twig becomes more violent as it creates scars on my palm. This way I'm the one hurting myself and not anything or anyone else. The little twig becomes tired and runs through my fingers. I let it go. At least it fulfilled the purpose of which I needed it for. I pinch my arm to get rid of the excess blood, then use water from the lake to clean my hands and arm. Steadily I start my journey back home, feeling better than when I arrived.

As the days pass by, so does the blood within my veins. Britney and I don't even look at each other in class, let alone speak. Anytime she tries to talk to me, I shove or ignore her. What's the point of even going to school? I'm never going to use most of this stuff in life, so I stop going to my classes. Every day I tell mom I'm going to take the bus, when all I really do is run into the woods and cut myself till I am pleased. Till the scars can hide the pain and the bruises can release the love. All the love I had for my family, Zach, and myself. Especially myself.

Summer is arriving fast and while girls my age are going to pool parties and the mall with their friends, I'm here in my room by myself.

"Shoot," I say to myself. "Stupid razor, you break so easily."

I trash the razor and put on a sweatshirt. Mom and Harry went out for something I don't care about, so I'm home alone on this sunny Sunday morning. I go downstairs to the kitchen searching for something to eat. Open a drawer and I find something much better than a razor. Hunger disappears and excitement fills my body. I grab the sharpest knife I see and even though I'm home alone, it's hidden under my sweatshirt. Once in my room, I quickly lock the door running into my bathroom, remove my sweatshirt and start using my new best friend. I'm dragging the knife slowly not only across my arms, but my thighs. Making straight, curvy and jagged lines on my body like art. Drawing circles and squares. Stars and diamonds. I turn on the water in my bathtub, put my legs in and continue cutting.

Chapter 5

"Where have you been?" Mom asks as I walk in. She's standing in the kitchen with the phone in her hand and a frown on her face.

"School" I say casually.

"Amelia Marie-Anne Zebororie, where have you been?" she yells.

"I told you, school."

"If you're coming back from school as you say, why did I just get a call from your guidance counselor explaining to me that you haven't been in school for the last TWO WEEKS and you missed school today" she shouts at me.

"Two weeks" she repeats frustrated. I look at her with no emotion, showing no sign of solace or apology.

"Are you even listening to me?" she asks.

"Yes, I heard what you said"

"Look Lia I'm done playing games with you. These days you're always coming in and out and staying in your room. You don't even go into the music room anymore. I thought you were still getting over Zack's death, but now I get a phone call from your school stating that you've missed two weeks of school and I'm starting to wonder if something's wrong. Lia, are you okay?" she finally stops looking into my eyes with her piercing blue eyes.

I ask myself if I should tell her. No way, she would never understand. Besides she has enough problems with her own life, I don't need to add to them. I tell her I'm fine and rush to my room. I start removing my sweatshirt when I hear her knocking on my door. I put it back on all the way and tell her to come in.

"Okay so first thing tomorrow," she says stroking my hair, "We'll make an appointment with your counselor and I will start driving and picking you up from school again."

I remove her hand and ask why. She gives me a look that says because I said so. I'm too tired to argue so I say okay even though I don't mean it. Then she tells me that I'm going to start eating dinner with her and Harry starting tonight. I nod in agreement to get her out of my room. Once she leaves, I start devising a plan on how I'm going to get out of school tomorrow. There's no way I'm going back, I can't go back. I take the knife from my bottom night stand drawer and go into my bathroom to release my anger.

"Hey, how are you?" Britney asks in homeroom. I stare at her for a minute wondering why she's talking to me.

"Fine" I reply. "Why are you talking to me?"

"It's been a long time since I've seen you and I wanted to know how you're doing." She says. "Why haven't you been coming to school?"

Silence fills the air.

"Listen I'm sorry for what I said and how I said those things the last time we talked. You had just lost someone close to you and I should have known better than to disturb you in your time of mourning" she says.

"I suppose I'm sorry too," the words choke me as I speak "for the way I acted."

"I called you to apologize, but you never picked up."

"I got a new phone and number"

"Okay, well I'll see you around." She turns and walks toward this group of girls. Maybe her new friends, maybe just girls she talks to during homeroom. Don't know, don't care.

When the bell rings, I take what seems like the usual path to my first class. I go into the first bathroom I see. Inside one of the stalls, I combine my savings of three hundred dollars with the seven hundred I took from mom's purse and put it in my wallet. Does she really think sending me back to school will solve anything? I take my cellphone out of my backpack and turn it on. It's the new one. The one Harry gave me for no reason. Love and happiness aren't in my vocabulary anymore. I hate the world and it hates me. I hate life and it hates me back. The late bell rings and I sneak out of the bathroom heading for a clear exit. I put my silent but deadly thoughts away.

Outside I walk to the student parking lot and see a familiar face getting into his car. Drew Lash, the popular senior who became class president earlier this year. Last year, he kept trying to ask me out even though he could get any other girl. I was too smart to let him into my life. Zack told me he was a player. I go up to his car. He sees me and smiles.

"Is that you Lia Zebororie?" he asks in his charming voice.

"Yeah, it's me" I say, "Why are you leaving now?"

"I'm done for this school year," he says, "I just came by to pick up something."

"Do you mind giving me a ride?"

"Aren't you supposed to be in class?"

"Please don't answer me with a question"

"Where to?" he asks.

I tell him anywhere as long as it's not nearby. I get in the car and we drive away. Twenty minutes later, I find myself in his home which is better than I expected. He lives with his older brother because their parents abandoned them, and his brother is the only one he has. It's a fairly large two bedroom condo with an awesome view of the city. Reasonably clean considering two guys live here.

"So what are you running away from?" Drew asks me while sitting on the couch with me.

"I really don't know." An awkward silence sustains.

"I heard about Zack, I'm sorry" he says.

"Don't be" I say as rapidly and sharply as I can. Another long awkward pause.

"How long do you want to stay?" he asks.

"A few days would be fine" I say, "thank you."

I lay my head on his shoulder and he asks me if I want to go out with him and his brother tomorrow tonight. I say yes, it's not like I had any plans before. He takes my stuff and I to his room when I tell him I need some sleep. After he leaves, I just lay there on his bed, wide awake.

I bring my backpack with me to the bathroom. I fell asleep two hours ago, but now I'm awake and have work to do. My phone starts ringing. I check the number and it's mom.

"What?" I answer cooly.

"Where are you?" she asks, "I've been out here since 2:30 PM"

"Oh I forgot to tell you," I start, "I'm going to spend two nights at Katrina's house."

"I thought you stopped talking to her." She says. "Are you sure because her mom didn't call me?"

"Yeah, I just forgot," I say, "I'm sorry. I haven't been myself lately, so I called her last night and asked if I could spend a few nights. I don't know why it slipped my mind. I'm so sorry." She asks me about extra clothes and other stuff, but I tell her I packed what I would need this morning.

"Are you sure you don't need anything else?" She asks.

"Yes, I'm sure" I tell her annoyed. "Oh and don't call her mom or dad. They went out for an important business meeting in Vegas so they won't pick up. Her older sister is staying with us."

"Okay" the naive woman says. "I guess I should say goodnight now. Don't stay up to late."

"I won't" I tell her, "goodnight."

I hang up and sigh in relief. I can't believe she bought that. I take out the knife from my bag and lock the bathroom door. "You no good, trouble making, life twisting girl" I say to myself while cutting. "You are such a liar and you deceive everyone. You don't care about anyone but yourself. You make life horrible for yourself and others around you." I push the knife harder into my thighs which makes blood gush out. The only reason I say things is to make me mad at myself. Then I can really hurt myself and have a reason for doing so. My body starts feeling weak so I stop. I wash off and go back to Drew's room for a night's rest.

The afternoon sunshine wakes me up with a headache. I decide to wash up. The only clothing I packed are two black tank tops, a dark blue pair of dolphin shorts, and a plain pair of regular ripped up jeans. After taking a shower, I put on the jeans and one of the black tanks with my sweatshirt. I search my bag for the black hair dye I recently bought. Got it. Taking the hair dye along with a pair of scissors and I give my hair a makeover. After dyeing it jet black, I cut it. Long hair has been really annoying these days, so I give myself a pixie style haircut.

"Much better" I tell my reflection. Then put on some dark eyeshadow. I go back to the room and lay on the bed. I look over at the alarm clock. It's only 3:30 PM. What else can I do. Drew comes in telling me his brother is coming home tonight.

"Whoa" he says when he looks up and sees me.

"What?"

"Your hair..." he stutters, "It's just so different."

"Yeah, well I felt like I needed to do something different with it" I say. "Where has your brother been?"

"Brian's been in Iraq for the last year and he's finally coming home today."

"That's awesome" I tell him. "Is that why we're going out tonight?"

"Yes, but first we need to get you an ID."

"Why can't I use my student ID?"

"We're going to an 18 and over club."

"Oh, but isn't creating a fake ID illegal."

"Only if you get caught" he says and walks out. I always thought of Drew as the good kid who never breaks the school rules, let alone the law. Guess I was wrong.

When Brian gets home, Drew introduces me to him as his girlfriend. Brian greets me politely and goes to his room to get ready.

"Why did you tell him I'm your girlfriend?" I ask Drew once Brian is out of sight.

"He won't let you stay unless you're someone I'm in a relationship with." He explains. "So for the time you stay you just have to pretend to be my girlfriend."

On our way into the club my stomach starts turning and my palms start getting sweaty fast. This is the first time I'm going to a club. Furthermore, I've never broken the law. Ever. I give my fake ID to the security guy. While he checks it, I start sweating even more. I hate sweating. I think he knows I'm a fake. He gives me back the card and lets me go in. What a rush.

I'm having the time of my life on the dance floor with Drew. Although he is starting to get sensual. I remove his hands and tell him no. After dancing for a while, my feet and head start hurting. I tell Drew I'm tired and he offers to drive me home. We find Brian and tell him that we're leaving. When we get home and I'm settled into bed, he offers me a shot glass of vodka.

"You do realize I'm only fifteen, right?" I ask him.

"I'm sorry, I thought after having the guts to sneak into a club with a fake id, you might have wanted to try some other things" he says. He stares at me for a while and gets up.

Before he leaves I jump out of bed, grab the glass and take it in one swallow. It tastes bitter and disgusting.

Ugh, why do people even drink this stuff. It sends a warm, fuzzy feeling down my throat and I get a little lightheaded.

"Are you okay?" Drew asks concerned.

"Yeah" I lie, "Never been better."

"Okay then," he says, "goodnight." He gives me a kiss on the cheek, turns and walks towards the door.

"Wait, you don't have to leave yet" I say walking up to him. I put my hands on his chest and give him a kiss on his soft lips. I never imagined having my first kiss with a guy who's last name I'm not even sure of. I let go of his soft lips. He cups my head and kisses me back. Before we know it, our short and innocent kisses turn into a make out session. He pulls away and starts to unbutton his shirt. Wait a minute, when did he get the wrong message. Apparently he knows I'm worried because he asks if I'm okay. I walk away from him and sit on the bed. He sits next to me and asks the most personal question ever. For the first time in a long while I say the truth.

"Just relax, it's no big deal" he says. He starts massaging my neck with his lips. I tell him to stop.

"How many girls have you brought in here?" I ask him looking into his eyes.

"Only you in the last two years" he says.

"Thanks for your honesty" I say getting up.

"Lia, I really care about you" he says holding on to my hand.

"You do?" I ask, stopping.

"Yeah" he says smiling at me.

"I have to tell you something" I say.

"What is it?" I roll up my sleeves and show him my scars.

"I cut" I tell him ashamed.

He tells me the scars don't change the way he feels about me and he's willing to get me the help I need.

Well, this is the first time I'm getting full attention since mom told me she's engaged. I'm not going to push away the only person giving me attention. Besides, he just told me he cares about me. He kisses me removing my sweatshirt, but I pull back.

"What's wrong now?"

I quickly think of an excuse and ask him if he has protection. He says no, but goes to his brother's room to get some. Crap. He starts kissing me again and I pull back.

"I need to wash the makeup on my face off first." I tell him.

Once in the bathroom, I pour cold water on my face and hair. I scrub the makeup off with my fingernails and a wet towel. I can't believe I'm going to go through with this. Am I really going to throw away all my morals tonight? Do I want to do this or am I making myself do this? Making myself do this to fill the emptiness within or to get attention. Am I making myself go through with this to express my anger towards mom? Is this an act of rebellion, rage or both? I pour more icy water on my face and get out of the bathroom. Drew asks if I'm okay. I tell him I'm fine even though I'm not and give myself to him.

Chapter 6

10:05 a.m. and I'm still in bed. I look to my left and see Drew.

"Good morning sunshine" he smiles. I put my hands on his bare chest.

"Are you going out today?"

"No," he says, "why?"

"I was just thinking, maybe we could stay in all day." I say then kiss him. He tackles me down and gets on top of me.

Suddenly we hear loud knocks on the outside. Drew gets up, and we both put on clothes to see who's at the front door. He opens the door and I see three people who have deep frowns on their faces. Only two I recognize.

"Ma'am is this your daughter?" the police officer asks mom before I can leave the room.

"Yes, that's her" she whispers. Brian comes out of his room confused.

"What's going on here?" he asks, looking at Drew and I.

The cop asks him if he's the one in charge here and Brian says yes. He then asks him how old he his.

All this while mom's staring at me with a blank face. I ask why as the cop puts Brian in handcuffs.

"He's the legal guardian here" he says. He then tells me both Drew and I have to go downtown with him.

"Why?" I ask again.

"Because that's the way things are done around here."

"How did you even know I was here?" I ask mom on our way out.

"The cellphone I gave you," Harry says, "has a tracking device on it so we know exactly where you are all the time. My daughter has one just like it."

"Lucky her" I say sarcastically.

"You should be thanking him." Mom says. "If it wasn't for that cellphone we wouldn't have known where you were. What were you thinking sneaking off with a guy to his place? I'll tell you what you were thinking, you weren't thinking at all because if you were you would have known that spending two nights in a condo with two grown men who could have hurt you is very stupid. They could have done bad things to you Lia. Maybe you wouldn't still be alive if we hadn't come on time. Even Emily who is in another state doesn't give me half as much trouble as you do."

Two days have gone by and I'm on my way to a rehabilitation center far away from Phoenix. After I confessed yesterday, Drew and his brother were able to go home. However I have to spend two months in captivity because mom says she can't handle me, but I know Harry told her to do it. For two months, no TV, music, or knives. How am I going to survive? When we get inside the building, a petite woman with long light brown hair in a dull brown dress approaches us. She talks to my mom for a while and collects my suitcases from her. Mom tries to hug me goodbye, but I don't let her. I follow the woman down a long white hallway and don't look back. Mom's watching me as I go. I can feel her eyes on my back, but I don't look back. I never look back.

When I finally get to the room I'll be staying in, there's nothing but four white walls and a plain looking bed. I ask the woman to give me my stuff. She says I'm not allowed to have any personal items with me and leaves. I immediately put her on my mental hate list. What kind of place is this? This isn't rehab, it's ten times worse than a regular center. There's not much to look at considering the walls are blank and the only furniture in here is a small bed with light blue sheets. I sit on the edge of the bed. I guess it all ends here. Just when I was starting to live and enjoy life again, it shuts me down and gives me pain and torture. What the hell is this life even about? Why on earth I'm I here? Why did

I run? How did I get myself into this mess? I roll up my sleeves. Shoot, I don't even have a knife. My nails are no good either. They're long, but not as long and sharp as a knife is. Ugh!

After spending two weeks in this prison designed as a treatment center, my arms are starting to heal and I'm learning how to fight the urge to cut or hurt myself. I'm lying in bed thinking about my progress when I hear a knock on my door. I tell the person to come in. I'm beyond shocked and surprised to see Britney open the door. She was the last person I saw before running away.

"Hey" she says sitting on the edge of the bed.

"Hi," I stutter, "what are you doing here?"

"Your mom told me you were here." She smiles. "How are you?"

"Better"

"So what happened," she asks, "to you?"

"It's a long story"

"Well, I'm going to be here for a while" she says, "Start talking."

Even though it's hard, I tell her everything. From my dad leaving to Zack's death. From mom's stupid engagement announcement to being totally isolated. I tell her about the plan I made to escape my house and how I stole money from my mom's purse. I tell her about the shot glass of vodka I took and the night

I spent with Drew. I tell her everything that occurred from the morning I got caught in my web of lies until this morning and she listens. She listens closely without interrupting or making facial expressions.

When I'm done, she doesn't walk away or tell me that I'm going to hell. She doesn't leave like I thought she would. Neither does she tells me God hates me or remind me of the things I've done. Instead she hugs and cries with me. She tells me she's here for me and I'm going to be okay. "I love you" are the words that come out of her mouth. She has to leave now, but she tells me she'll be back soon. I look forward to seeing her again.

Chapter 7

Britney comes to visit me for the rest of the week. We talk, laugh, and at times cry together. Time passes quickly when she's around. Every morning I wake up and long for her to come and when she leaves, I reflect on our time spent together.

I get to leave the center for the Independence Day celebration. Britney and her family come to pick me up after asking mom for permission. We spend the day at the amusement park riding different roller coasters. Britney and I go on all of them even though her parents didn't want us to. When the night arrives with its gorgeous beauty and weather, we walk towards the Ferris wheel to see the fireworks. The perfect ending to a spectacular day.

Days later, mom visits. After leaving me here alone for weeks, she finally visits me. Our conversation turns out dry based on the fact that I give her one word answers to her questions. Ten minutes go by and she leaves frustrated with me. Oh well.

The day after mom visits, Emily comes. She tells me she came back from Berkley yesterday.

"When I didn't see you I asked mom where you were and she practically told me every detail of what happened."

"So why are you here?" I ask her.

"To get your side of what happened" she says.

"Why?" I ask. "So you can go report to mom what her least favorite child said."

"No sweetie. I just want to know the truth and I am not her favorite child."

"You swear you won't tell mom or Harry."

"I swear," she says. "Besides I don't even talk to Harry."

"Well, after Zack died I just felt depressed, like my only reason for living just left and I didn't need mom getting engaged for money. It was like everything bad that could possibly happen was happening to me and since you were busy in school, I couldn't talk to you. I felt extremely alone and I felt like nobody cared. There was Britney, but she's a Jesus freak and I didn't want anything to do with her. I blamed her for Zack's death and I was angry at her so I started cutting myself. When I felt irritated or sad, instead of crying or screaming. I would cut. I cut to see blood, hoping the more blood that came out, the closer to death I would be. I even cut when I didn't need to. Sometimes I would spray perfume or put some rubbing alcohol on the open cuts to get them infected. I was desperate to hurt myself in any way I could. I also stopped going to school and when mom found out she freaked. The next morning she forced me to go to school, but I didn't want to go back. I sneaked out of class and asked Drew for a ride. Spent two nights in his home, went to an 18 and over club, got his brother arrested and that's about it. You've gotta believe me, Em. I only did these things because I was lonely I wasn't trying to hurt or get anyone in trouble."

"I believed you up until to the part about you spending two nights at Drew's condo" she says. "Did you really sleep there after what Zack and I told you about him."

"He was the only one who was there for me." I say not looking directly at her.

"You did not."

"He was really sweet to me and it wasn't like you were around for me to talk to."

"You should have called me" she says. "I can't believe you slept with him."

"God, you know I told Britney the same thing and she didn't say anything like that."

"I'm sorry" she says. "I should have been there for you, I'm really sorry."

I tell her it wasn't her fault and she lies in the bed with me looking up at the ceiling. She tells me as sisters we need to stick together, especially now that mom got married. I can't believe she got remarried. After all the signs I gave her, she still went ahead and got married. Now there's no chance of my family getting back together.

Chapter 8

I only have a few more days to go, but I have to spend my birthday here since Britney and her family are in Miami for vacation and mom has probably forgotten about me. I can't believe I'm spending my sixteenth birthday alone. A girl's sweet sixteen is supposed to be the defining time of her teenage years. Emily bursts through the door with a big smile on her face saying happy sweet sixteen Lia. I get out of bed to hug her, but see another surprise at the door. I start crying as he walks towards me.

"Is that really you Dad?" I ask.

"Yeah, it's me Lia" he says in the once familiar tone. I see his tears for the first time as he asks me to forgive him.

"Yes, I forgive you" I tell him hugging him. Emily joins us and I think of the last time I was in a family hug like this. Dad and Em tell me they're taking me out for my birthday.

"Does mom know about this?" I ask them.

"Yeah, dad came back home yesterday and after

he apologized they talked it over."

"So you and mom are okay now?" I ask my dad.

"Yes, but keep talking and we won't have time to have any fun today" he says.

I stop talking and we head out for fun filled day. So glad I don't have to spend my birthday alone and in rehab. We go to the state fair which is one of my favorite ways to start summer. I tell my dad how much I missed him while eating lunch with him, Em and her boyfriend, who's really a great guy that I never got a chance to know.

"So I guess you met Harry right?"

"I did" he says. "Likable guy."

"Dad you don't have to lie to me" I tell him.

"I'm not lying," he says, "he's going to take care of your mom, sister and you. Unlike me, he won't leave you guys."

"Nobody's perfect"

"I know but that's the worst decision I ever made."

I ask him if I can live with him after I get out of rehab.

"No way" he says.

"Why?"

"Because I'm not stable right now and you'll have a better life living with your mom and Harry."

"Yeah cause that worked out so well the first time."

I get up and walk away. I can't believe after

everything I've been through, my dad is going to send me back to the home (which it even isn't anymore) he and mom built together, but is now being lived in by another man and his daughter just tears me apart inside. This is all mom's fault. If she hadn't married the dude, our family could be back together by now.

My two months in the "treatment center" are over today, but I'm not going home today. I'm staying in Britney's house for a while. I deserve to be happy. I deserve to be where I feel loved and wanted. A place where I'm not in solitary.

After unpacking in her house, Britney and I go down to her pool to relax. It's hard to believe that eleven months ago I wanted nothing to do with the girl, but now we're side by side hanging out at her pool. Who would have thought she'd end up being one of my friends, my best friend for that matter. She really has helped me with forgiveness, letting go of pain and finding myself.

"Britney?" She looks at me with innocence.

"Yeah"

"Why didn't you leave when I pushed you away?" I ask her. "What kept you staying?"

"I never give up on God's people. If God loves you, who am I not to. He loves us so much, He sent His Son, Jesus to die for us."

"I know you're a Jesus freak and all that, but I seriously don't need or want to be part of any kind of religion" I tell her.

"Knowing who Jesus is isn't about religion" she says. "It's about a lifelong relationship."

Chapter 9

Since that day at the pool, I've been learning more about God and His eternal love for me. My life has drastically changed positively. It's like I've been searching for something my whole life and finally found it. For so long I had been fighting hands who just wanted to hold me. Love that is true and pure. I don't think I can ever live without this kind of love in my life. This love was what was missing in my life. If I had experienced this kind of love earlier, I wouldn't have done any of what I've done.

I still have trouble understanding why God would send His only Son to die for humanity and why would Jesus agree. He could have told God no, I don't want to die for them. He could have asked God why do I have to die for sinners who take your name in vain. People who worship idols instead of You. Yet He didn't say that. Jesus never said any of that and even when the pain was too much for Him, He kept going because that's how much He loves us. That's how much He loves me. When He died, He died for everyone. It's not like He told God He was only dying for a specific group of people. On the cross He said, "Father, forgive them, for they do not know what they are doing." He didn't say Father only forgive the thieves, or the liars or even the idol worshipers. He asked God to forgive all of us even when He had been nailed to the cross. I've never seen or heard of a love like that. Now I know why Britney is a Jesus freak.

Emily and my dad start coming to church with me. Though he doesn't live in Phoenix anymore, my dad makes an effort to be there for Emily and I. Every time he takes Em and I out for dinner, he reminds us that we're all in this together. We're all in together towards learning more about Jesus and living our new lives. My new church family and Britney are also guiding me through life. She is literally the angel God sent to me and her family has been nothing but splendid and patient with me. I'm grateful she didn't leave me alone even when I told her to. Since I let Jesus have my heart and life, Britney, her family and her church have been there for me. They've let me know I'm not alone. Living the true Christian life isn't easy, especially getting rid of my bad habits and learning how to forgive those who have hurt me.

Even though I know I've been forgiven, my past still haunts me. At night, the horrible memories creep up and surround me reminding me that I will never be free from my past. Britney told me this would happen. She said when it happens I have to pray to God, but how can I pray when I feel so bad about myself. I can't pray knowing God knows my dirty little secrets. How do I know He still loves me after everything I've done? I guess that's why He sent Jesus, because He still loves me even though He has seen me at my worst. So when the memories come knocking at my door, I pray for the strength, and love, and forgiveness towards myself and others. I can't live holding on to what mom, my dad, Emily, and so many others have done to me. I have to forgive myself or I'll never be able to let Jesus completely into my life. I have to forgive myself and let the past go. I have to learn to trust Jesus with my life. Every night, when depression seems to be just outside the window of my heart, I pray. I pray with everything I have, with all the faith I have hoping God is listening. I pray for the strength to live, hope to love, and help to forgive. These next few years are not going to be easy at all, but Jesus was willing to die for me even though He didn't have to. So to say I can't or won't follow Him after all He has done for me would be like denying myself the best life experience and friend in the world. I want a relationship with Him and no matter what happens or what anyone says I will always follow Jesus.

I have to go back to my house today now that I'm much better. I was only staying at Britney's so I wouldn't be alone. I say goodbye to my Britney and her family. As they drop me off at my house, I tell them I'll see them in church on Sunday. I'm truly laughing and I can't stop smiling. I even skip like a five year old to the front steps to ring the doorbell. Emily opens the door with open arms excited to see me. She hugs me in a way she never has before and tells me how happy she is to see me back home again. She takes my bags and welcomes me back home.

"Where's mom?" I ask Em once I'm settled in.

"With Harry." She tells me they've been out all day with a disgusted tone.

"I'm going outside for a walk" I tell her.

"You're going to walk in the rain?" I look outside in disbelief and see that it is raining.

I rush out the front door and run as fast as I can to the lake. It's ironic that this is the same day, August 30, when it rained last year. I'm in the same spot I was a year ago and this is also the first rainfall of the summer. I take this as a sign that Zack is watching me from up above. As much as I miss him I'm at peace knowing that he is in a much better place.

Over the last twelve months I lost a friend and myself. I've hurt myself in many ways, stole, lied, broke the law, and almost killed myself. Yet I also found a friend who was willing to tell me the truth in a loving way. I had to go through all this just to find eternal love. Love that will never leave me. The kind of love that never ends even when I've lost my way. Britney once said sometimes non pleasurable things happen, not because God is trying to punish anyone, but to show us that we can't help ourselves and to glorify Him. He always brings the good out of the bad. I should be dead. I shouldn't be alive. However I thank God I am.

I let go. I let go of the pain. I let go of the trauma my father caused. I let go of the heartache from Zack's death. I let everything go and feel the *august rain*. I finally forgive my mom. I forgive Drew for taking advantage of me though I gave myself to him. I forgive myself for the damage I've caused. If God can take me, a sinner who never believed in Him and never wanted Him in my life, I make up my mind that there's no sin horrible that can separate anyone from Him. His love has truly set me free. Looking up to the sky, soaked in the soothing rain, I smile knowing that God will take care of me. I can finally breathe, knowing everything will be okay. I'm in better hands now.

About The Author

Dunamis Ore is currently a 17 year old homeschooled senior, who takes group classes at Shabach Christian Academy. She has a passion for acting and writing which started in 2nd grade. However, she was inspired by her 5th grade teacher to start writing more. She began writing this book for fun towards the end of her last year in middle school until she was recently advised to publish it for a wider audience. Dunamis currently lives with her parents and siblings in Maryland.

Contact Information

Dunamis Ore would love to get your feedback, feel free to contact her using the mediums listed below.

Dunamis Ore
Kingdom Ambassadors Christian Center
9475 Lottsford Road, Suite 110
Largo, MD 20774
USA

Phone: 301-494-5400
Email: augustrainbook@gmail.com
Website: www.dunamisore.com
Twitter: twitter.com/dunamisore

You can order additional copies of this book @

www.daforge.com
www.amazon.com
www.barnesandnoble.com

Scan the QR code to visit dunamisore.com

Other Projects by Dunamis Ore

In 6th grade, I was blessed to be part of my middle school's play, **Oliver**! I loved being part of the cast. I was really shy back then, but I thought it would be nice to step out of my shell and audition. That was the first real play I had done and I loved the backstage treatment of getting hair and make-up done during the nights we performed.

In 2008, I took classes at **John Robert Powers**, a prestige school for actors, singers, and models. I absolutely LOVED the experience and learned a lot about myself. My confidence grew and it was an honor to have Ms. Arnetia Walker as one of my teachers who I learned commercial techniques from. I also learned dialects from Ms. Rhoads who was just a bundle of joy to work with! I also loved working with the other students. I'll never forget those few months. So much fun!

I became part of the cast for **Cats**, one of my favorite musicals till this day, when I was 12 years old. It was during the summer of 2008 in a community theater close to where my family and I used to live. Being a "cat" required full on costume and make-up which I loved because that's one of my favorite things about portraying a character. I made friends and got along with everyone who was part of the project, which wasn't hard because they were all so friendly and welcoming.

During the summer of 2009, I went back to LMP, my local community theater for their annual youth play which was **Rogers and Hammerstein's Cinderella**. I loved being there again and seeing the friends I made from the previous summer. That summer was so much fun! I remember running up to my room and crying behind the closed door after I got home from the last show. It was too sad to see the show come to an end.

THE TOUCHSTONE MOVIE

In 2011, I decided to take a break from theater and find a role in **The Touchstone** movie since I want to be a TV/film actress. In August, I was blessed enough to be part of a film which was shot in Virginia. This was a whole new experience that I absolutely loved! I would only wake up at 5 am to do something that I love. I wasn't even getting paid but I still went in with excitement because of how much fun I was having on and off set. On the last day of shooting for me, I was there by 12 noon and didn't come back home till 12:30 am the next day! It was worth it though because I had so much fun with the rest of the cast and it was an awesome experience.